IRMA

The Flying Bowling Ball

by **TOM ROSS**

illustrated by **REX BARRON**

G. P. PUTNAM'S SONS   NEW YORK

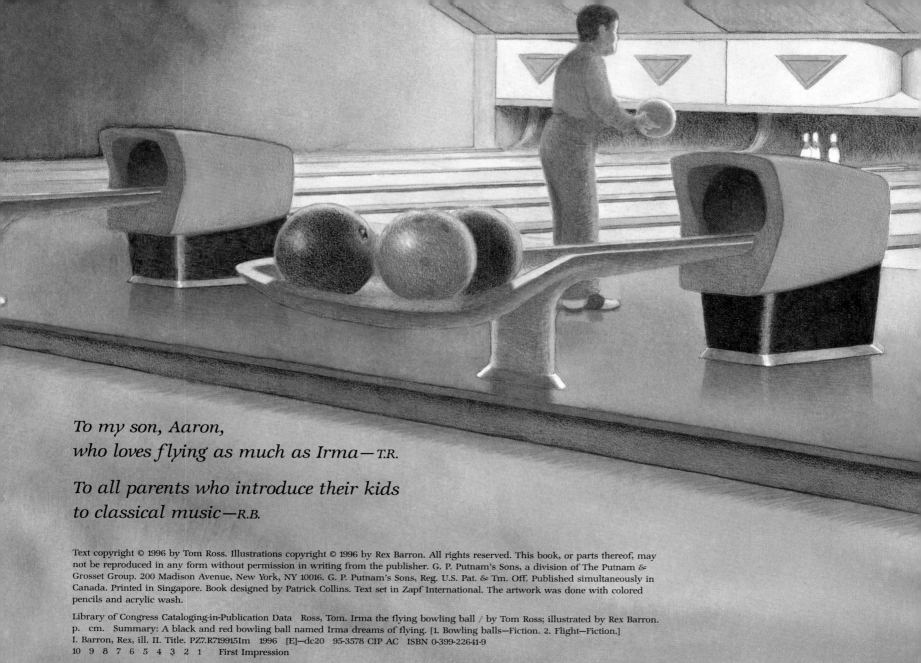

To my son, Aaron,
who loves flying as much as Irma—T.R.

To all parents who introduce their kids
to classical music—R.B.

Text copyright © 1996 by Tom Ross. Illustrations copyright © 1996 by Rex Barron. All rights reserved. This book, or parts thereof, may not be reproduced in any form without permission in writing from the publisher. G. P. Putnam's Sons, a division of The Putnam & Grosset Group. 200 Madison Avenue, New York, NY 10016. G. P. Putnam's Sons, Reg. U.S. Pat. & Tm. Off. Published simultaneously in Canada. Printed in Singapore. Book designed by Patrick Collins. Text set in Zapf International. The artwork was done with colored pencils and acrylic wash.

Library of Congress Cataloging-in-Publication Data   Ross, Tom. Irma the flying bowling ball / by Tom Ross; illustrated by Rex Barron.
p. cm.   Summary: A black and red bowling ball named Irma dreams of flying. [1. Bowling balls—Fiction. 2. Flight—Fiction.]
I. Barron, Rex, ill. II. Title. PZ7.R719915Im   1996   [E]—dc20 95-3578 CIP AC   ISBN 0-399-22641-9
10 9 8 7 6 5 4 3 2 1   First Impression

There once was a red and black bowling ball named Irma.

She rode in a sleek blue carrying case and got
polished every week. For a bowling ball, Irma had
a pretty good life.

Irma felt proud to belong to a professional bowler,
and she tried her best to shoot for the strikes. Together
they won lots of tournaments.

One day, however, everything changed. Irma saw
a strange sight outside the living room window. "My
heavens," she thought. "A flying bowling ball."

From then on, all Irma could think about was that flying bowling ball. Irma wanted to fly too. Because her head was in the clouds, her scores suffered terribly.

Irma began to mess up in every tournament.

Finally her owner had no choice but to trade her in for a new ball.

Irma was placed on a rack with the cracked and beat-up bowling balls. She had no idea what was happening to her.

The next day all sorts of strange hands pawed and poked at her.

A little boy spilled his Coke, and left Irma dripping. "I can't stand it here," Irma moaned.

"Don't cry, hon," said Bunny, the dull, scratched ball beside her. "You just got to take the hard knocks with the bounces."

"If only I could fly," Irma sighed.

Bunny laughed. "Fly! Bowling balls can't fly!"

Irma's heart sank, as a little girl grabbed her. Would she spend the rest of her life bounced from stranger to stranger? No! There had to be more!

Suddenly the little girl lost her grip and Irma
slipped free—and crashed through the window.
"Oh my, I'm flying!" Irma screamed.

Lucky for her, Farmer Pete saw her just in time.
Irma went spiraling into the back of his old pickup
stacked with springy mattresses. "Whoa!" she yodeled,
zinging back into the air.

At Gus's Gas, she scored a strike.

Then she struck it rich.

"How do you get down from here?" Irma shouted
to a bird. Now she wondered whether this flying
business was such a good idea after all.

All of a sudden, the pump slowed down and Irma
was rolling again. "Phew!" she said. "On the road again."

Soon Irma was back to what she did best—
knocking into things.

Her world was beginning to seem topsy-turvy.

Finally Irma settled down and could enjoy flying at last. "This is more like it!" she thought. Irma enjoyed the afternoon sun and the cool ocean breeze. She now realized that almost anything is possible if you set your mind to it. "Bowling balls can't fly, huh?"

A few days later, after hundreds of trips going around and around, Irma grew a bit restless. She stared off into the distance at the children playing on a beach beyond the park. Then something caught her eye. Round, with yellow and red stripes reflecting the sun, it bounced and floated in the waves.

"A *swimming* bowling ball?" Irma thought. Hmmmmmm.